Name : ....

Class : ....Roll No. ....

Sec. : ....

School : ....

MANOJ PUBLICATIONS

Rhymes For Junior K.G.

Songs For Junior K.G.

JOHNY, JOHNY

Johny, Johny,
Yes, Papa.
Eating sugar ?
No, Papa.
Telling a lie ?
No, Papa.
Open your mouth,
Ha! Ha! Ha!

O GIRAFFE, GIRAFFE !

O Giraffe, Giraffe,
You make me laugh!
You are so tall
With a head so small!
You are so wrong
To have a neck so long!
O Giraffe, Giraffe,
You make me laugh!

HUMPTY DUMPTY

Humpty Dumpty sat on a wall,
Humpty Dumpty had a great fall.
All the King's horses
and all the King's men,
Could not put Humpty Dumpty
together again.

TEDDY BEAR, TEDDY BEAR

Teddy bear, Teddy bear,
Turn around;
Teddy bear, Teddy bear,
Touch the ground.
Teddy bear, Teddy bear,
Polish your shoes;
Teddy bear, Teddy bear,
Off to school.

RAIN, RAIN, GO AWAY
Rain, rain, go away,
Come again another day;
Little Johny wants to play,
Rain, rain go away.

HICKORY, DICKORY, DOCK

Hickory, Dickory, Dock,
The mouse ran up the clock.
The clock struck one,
The mouse ran down,
Hickory, Dickory, Dock.

DING, DONG, BELL

Ding, dong, bell,
Pussy's in the well;
Who put her in ?
Little Tommy Thin.
Who pulled her out ?
Little Johny Stout.
What a naughty boy was that
To drown poor pussy cat!

ONE, TWO, BUCKLE MY SHOE

One, two,
Buckle my shoe;
Three, four,
Shut the door;
Five, six,
Pick up sticks;
Seven, eight,
Lay them straight;
Nine, ten,
A big fat hen.

RING-A-RING O' ROSES

Ring-a-ring o' roses,
A pocket full of posies,
Hush-ha! Bush-ha!
We all fall down.

MARY HAD A LITTLE LAMB

Mary had a little lamb,
Its fleece was white as snow,
And everywhere that Mary went
The lamb was sure to go.
It followed her to school one day,
Which was against the rule;
It made the children laugh and play
To see a lamb at school.

PUSSY CAT, PUSSY CAT

Pussy cat, pussy cat,
where have you been ?
I have been to London,
to visit the Queen.
Pussy cat, pussy cat,
what did you there ?
I frightened a little mouse,
under the chair.

CHUBBY CHEEKS

Chubby cheeks, dimpled chin,
Rosy lips, teeth within,
Curly hair, very fair,
Eyes are blue, lovely too,
Teacher's pet, is that you ?
Yes, Yes, Yes !

MY SPECIAL HOME

Some houses are big,
Some houses are small,
Some houses are wide,
Some houses are tall.

So many houses,
Wherever I roam;
The very best one
Is my own special home.

COCK-A-DOODLE DOO!

Cock-a-doodle doo!
My dame has lost her shoe,
My master's lost his fiddling stick,
And knows not what to do.

ROCK-A-BYE BABY

Rock-a-bye baby,
On a tree-top,
When the wind blows,
The cradle will rock.
When the bough breaks,
The cradle will fall,
Down will come baby,
Cradle and all!

POLLY PUT THE KETTLE ON

Polly put the kettle on,
Polly put the kettle on,
Polly put the kettle on,
We will all have tea.
Sukey take it off again,
Sukey take it off again,
Sukey take it off again,
They have all gone home.

LITTLE BO-PEEP

Little Bo-peep has lost her sheep,
And doesn't know where to find them;
Leave them alone, and they will come home,
Bringing their tails behind them.

YOU SHALL HAVE AN APPLE

You shall have an apple,
You shall have a plum,
You shall have a rattle,
When your dad comes home.

JACK BE NIMBLE

Jack be nimble,
Jack be quick,
Jack jumps over
The candlestick.

LONDON BRIDGE IS FALLING DOWN

London Bridge is falling down,
Falling down, falling down,
London Bridge is falling down,
My fair lady.
Build it up with iron bars,
Iron bars, iron bars,
Build it up with iron bars,
My fair lady.

LITTLE TOMMY TUCKER

Little Tommy Tucker
sing for his supper;
What shall we give him ?
White bread and butter.
How shall he cut it
without any knife ?
How will he marry
without any wife ?

LITTLE MISS MUFFET

Little Miss Muffet,
Sat on a tuffet,
Eating her curds and whey.
There came a big spider,
Who sat down beside her,
And frightened Miss Muffet away.

ROSES ARE RED

Roses are red,
Violets are blue,
Sugar is sweet,
And so are you.

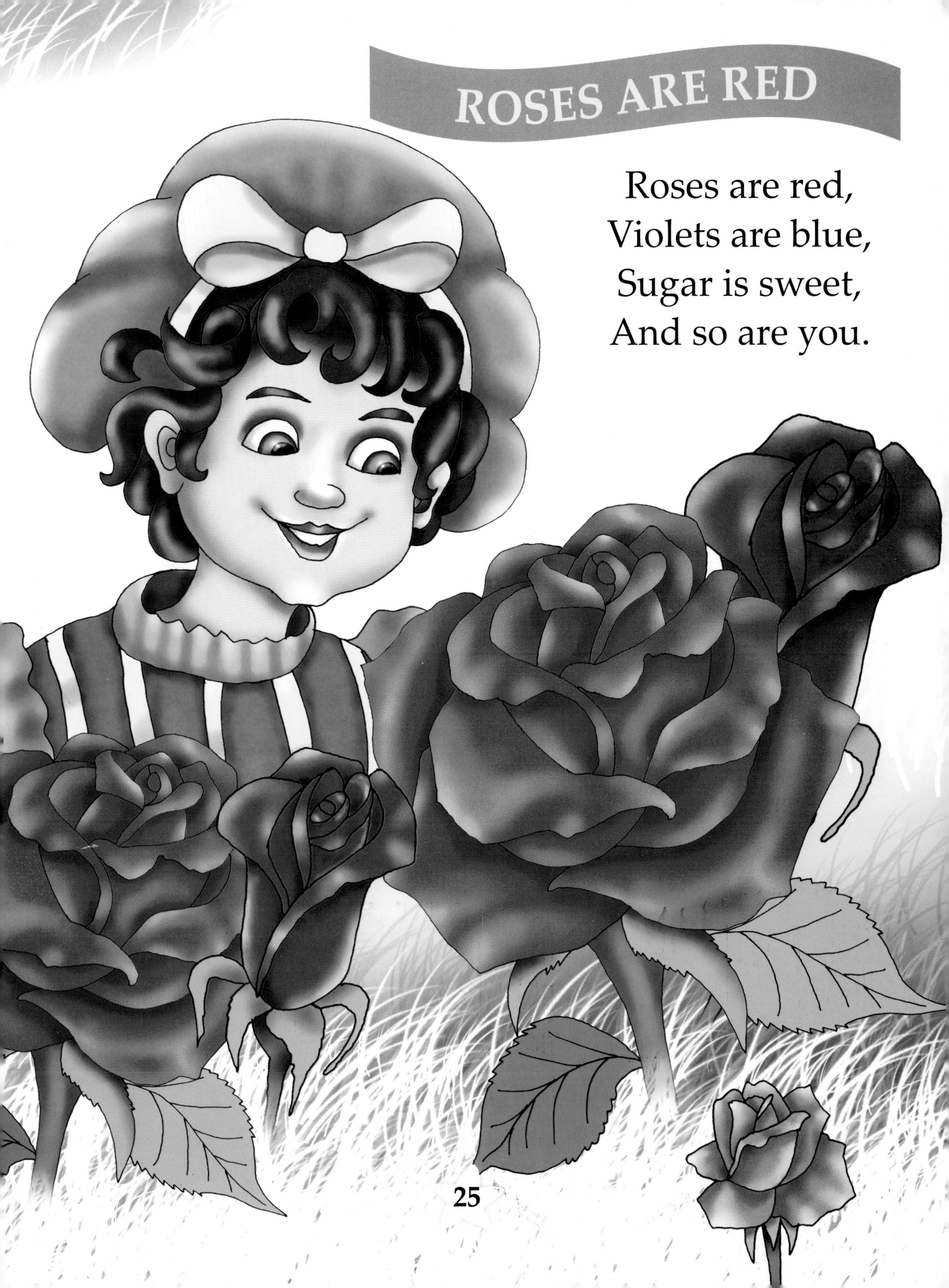

MARY, MARY

Mary, Mary, quite contrary,
How does your garden grow ?
With silver bells and cockle shells,
And pretty maids all in a row.

SEE-SAW

See-saw, up and down,
Which is the way to London town ?
One foot up, and the other foot down,
That is the way to London town.

BAA, BAA, BLACK SHEEP

Baa, baa, black sheep,
have you any wool ?
Yes sir, yes sir, three bags full.
One for my master, one for his dame,
And one for the little boy who lives down the lane.

TWINKLE, TWINKLE, LITTLE STAR

Twinkle, twinkle, little star,
How I wonder what you are !
Up above the world so high,
Like a diamond in the sky !

JACK AND JILL

Jack and Jill went up the hill.
To fetch a pail of water;
Jack fell down and broke his crown,
And Jill came tumbling after.

MY RED BALLOON

My red balloon, My red balloon,
Flies up, up, to the sky.
I jump up high, and try to fly,
But can't, oh tell me why ?
My red balloon, My red balloon,
Flies up, up, to the sky.

LITTLE JACK HORNER

Little Jack Horner, sat in a corner,
Eating a Christmas pie.
He put in his thumb,
And pulled out a plum,
And said, "What a good boy am I !"